Terry Lowell

My Zombie
Best Friend

Acknowledgements

Thank you to Janet Kelly and the team at Bobaloo Books for your belief in Gurr, and for all your support and hard work in making this book a reality.

Thank you Sam Porter for your patience, and for your fantastic illustrations.

A big thank you to Sue Matthews for your insightful editing and brilliant suggestions on how to make the story better. Don't try those spit balls at home.

A special thank you to Miss Ward and Class 5-1 Charles II of Netherhall Junior School, Huddersfield. You were my first editors, and your enthusiasm for Gurr and his friends gave me the encouragement to write 'more words'.

The biggest thank you is for Alison, my best critic and biggest fan. You have always been there, and I could not do what I do without you.

Dedication

For Nathan. My inspiration.

Chapter 1

"Stay away from there! They're dangerous!" Mum said. "They're rotten, they spread disease and they eat people!"

I'd watched from my bedroom window last night as our new neighbours moved into Mrs Wilson's old house. She was poorly and had gone to live with her son in Wales, and the house had been empty for six weeks. I was excited to see someone new moving in.

It was dark and the street light outside our house hadn't worked for ages, so I hadn't been able to see much of the new family as I spied on them unloading stuff from a large van. I could make out two grown-ups and what could have been a boy about my size, but not much more. I hoped he was nice. It would be good having someone my age in the street. All the other houses nearby were filled with old people or young couples with babies. That's why I'd made up my mind to go over and say hello before I went to school. And that's when Mum told me exactly who, or what, had moved in next door.

"Don't go anywhere near that house," she screeched, peering through a gap in the living room curtains. "I'll be talking to the council, mark my words. Having that sort in a decent street. It shouldn't be allowed. They wouldn't move a family like that next door to the mayor!"

Buzby jumped into my lap as I ate breakfast and I fed him a piece of bacon. Normally Mum would tell me off for feeding the dog from the table, but this morning she was too busy ranting about who she was going to complain to, which seemed to be everyone from the Queen down.

I grabbed my bag, nuzzled Buzby, shouted 'bye to Mum and headed for the bus stop. Blake was already there.

"Nathan! Have you seen 'em?"

"Seen who?" I said, knowing exactly who he meant.

"Them!" He lowered his voice and looked over his shoulder as if afraid of being overheard. "Our cat didn't come home last night. Dad says they ate it."

"Your cat's always wandering off," I said. "It lived at our house for three months!"

Blake shrugged. "Yea, well. They could've eaten it."

The bus arrived and we got on. We lived near the start of the route so me and Blake always got the back seat. We stared at my neighbours' house and the dark windows seemed to watch as we rode past.

"Dad says they only come out at night," Blake whispered.

I laughed. "They're not vampires."

"No, because vampires are not real," Blake said. "But they are. I get the creeps just thinking about 'em."

As the bus filled up it seemed I'd never been so popular. Even kids I'd never spoken to before wanted to talk to me. The subject was always the same. What were they like? Could I smell them? Was I scared?

It was fun being the centre of attention and I answered the questions as best I could. I hadn't met them, I couldn't smell them and I wasn't scared. People didn't believe me.

"Not scared!" Laura Mosley said. "How can you not be scared? What if they break into your house one day and… ugh!" She shuddered.

It was as if the mere thought of what they'd do if they broke into my house was just too horrible to talk about.

I'd thought Mum was exaggerating, but by the time we reached school I was beginning to wonder if everyone was right. Maybe I should be scared.

After all, it had to be dangerous living next door to a family of zombies.

Chapter 2

Maths was my favourite subject and I was calculating the area of a triangle when I realised my work group had gone quiet. As the other two in my group were Michelle and Raees that was almost a miracle. They never stopped talking. If talking was an international sport, they'd both be gold medallists. I heard Miss Ward clear her throat.

"Class. This is Gary," she said.

I looked up and there at the front of the class stood a boy. He wasn't like any boy I'd seen before. He was terribly thin and his brand new school uniform hung off him like an old suit on a scarecrow. His arms dangled inside baggy sleeves, and ended in withered hands and gnarled fingers. His slender neck stuck out from his collar, and his head perched on the end like a lolly on a stick. He was mostly bald with tufts of grey hair on the top of his head and over one ear. He only had one ear.

The boy looked at the class and the class looked at the boy. The paper-like skin on his face tightened as he moved his mouth. He was trying to smile but the effort just revealed two rows of rotting teeth in a hideous grimace. Some of his teeth were missing. The ones that remained were black.

I glanced around at the rest of the class. We all knew about zombies but this was the first time any of us had seen one up close. Laura's nose wrinkled in disgust. Blake's eyes were wide, as if he couldn't believe what he was seeing, and the rest of the class sat shocked, their mouths hanging open. There was a quiet shuffle as those closest slowly edged away.

"Gary has just moved into the area and is going to be in our class," Miss Ward said. She rested her right hand on the newcomer's shoulder. There were gasps from some of the other children. Miss Ward had actually touched a zombie. No one touched zombies. Didn't she know how dangerous that was?

"Despite what some of you may have heard about the Previously Infected, Gary and his family are completely cured and are no risk to anyone." Very deliberately, as if to emphasise her point, Miss Ward placed her left hand on the boy's other shoulder. She let her gaze move steadily across each child. "I know you will all make him feel welcome." It was an order rather than a request. "Nathan."

I started. Miss Ward had said my name. Why had she said my name?

"I understand you live next door to Gary. I'm sure you'll be great friends. Would you look after him? Show him where to go for lunch… that sort of thing?"

I opened my mouth but no words came out. I didn't know what to say. My teacher was telling me to be his friend but Mum had told me to stay away from him. What was I going to do?

Luckily it seemed Miss Ward didn't need an answer. She just smiled, showed the boy to the seat next to mine and went back to writing formulas on the board.

Behind us, Laura whispered. "You stink."

The boy ignored Laura and I ignored him, turning my attention quickly back to my maths book. I felt a nudge on my arm. I focussed on an equation and wrote down a couple of numbers which I immediately scribbled out. I couldn't concentrate. I felt another nudge and turned my head. The boy was holding out his hand to shake mine.

"Gurr," he said.

"Gurr?"

He pointed at himself. "Gurr."

He pushed his hand closer. Reluctantly I took it. Shaking his hand was like holding chicken bones wrapped in cling film. "Nathan," I said.

There was a snort. "Can't even say its own name," Laura whispered. "Freak."

Shaun stifled a laugh and I knew the other kids were watching to see what I'd do. Blake wrote something on a sheet of paper and, grinning, he held it up for me to see.

"Z.B.F." it said. Zombie best friend.

The bell went. We all gathered our books and headed for the corridor. Gurr was behind me so I hurried on, caught up with Blake and ran outside. Gurr could find his own way to the dining room.

Miss Ward hadn't mentioned to the other teachers that I was supposed to be looking after Gurr, so for the rest of the day I avoided him. If he sat at the front of the class, I sat at the back. If he sat at the back, I sat at the front. If he sat in the middle, I got as far away from him as possible. It wasn't easy because no one wanted to sit next to Gurr. Wherever he sat, the chairs in front, behind and to his sides were empty or dragged further away. He was like a lonely island in a sea of children.

In Art I heard Laura whispering "Zombie. Zombie. Zombie," just loud enough for Gurr to hear, and Tyler flicked him with paint leaving blue splashes down his new blazer. In History Shaun knocked Gurr's books onto the floor, and in Science Alex fired spit balls at his head.

Some of the teachers must have seen what was happening but they didn't say anything. I even noticed Mr Webster glare as he passed Gurr in the corridor.

I felt a bit sorry for Gurr, but not enough to interfere. Maybe that night he'd tell his mum and dad that school was awful and they'd move away. That would make a lot of people happy. But if he did stay, no doubt some loser would take pity on him. It just wouldn't be me.

I wasn't going to be a zombie's best friend. No way.

Chapter 3

The taunting continued on the bus home, and Laura and Shaun stayed on well past their stops because they were having so much fun.

"Zombie! Zombie! Zombie!" they sang, while Shaun tore pages out of his exercise books to screw up and throw at Gurr's head.

"Stop it now," I said. "You're just being mean."

Laura pointed at Gurr then at me, and began a new chant. "Z.B.F. Z.B.F."

Blake and Shaun took up the chant. "Z.B.F. Z.B.F."

I sank into my seat. Gurr wasn't my Z.B.F.

Eventually the bus reached our stop and we all got off. Gurr walked in front of us. Stiff-legged, his upper body rolled with every step, as if on a ship in a heavy storm. Shaun and Laura fell in behind Gurr, mimicking his walk and laughing.

"That's just nasty," I said. Blake seemed to agree, because he slowed to walk with me. I opened my mouth to shout at Laura, but at that moment she stuck out a foot to clip Gurr's ankles.

Gurr tripped, stumbled and fell, and as he hit the ground... his head fell off.

We stared, open-mouthed, as Gurr's head bounced past us, splashing everyone in rust-coloured goo. An eyeball popped from its socket, rolled across the pavement and came to rest against Laura's shoe. It rocked back and stared up at her.

Laura screamed, Blake screeched, Shaun shrieked and all three raced off in different directions.

Gurr pushed himself onto his knees and started feeling the ground with his hands. His head had ended up under a hedge and I could see he wasn't going to find it. Taking a deep breath, I gripped a thin tuft of hair and lifted Gurr's head, like a medieval executioner displaying a gory trophy. It swung in my grasp and Gurr's face turned to mine. With his one good eye, he winked.

I felt the gorge rise in my throat and for a moment I thought I was going to throw up. I swallowed hard. Holding the head as far away from me as possible, I took a step forward and shoved it into Gurr's chest. Gurr took the head, lifted it onto the thin stalk of his neck and snapped it back in place. He stood up.

"Thnk," he said, picking up his eyeball and pushing it into the socket.

"You're welcome," I said and we stayed for a moment, just staring at each other. "Does it hurt?" I asked at last.

Gurr shook his head. It was a gentle shake, as if he was afraid his head would fall off again.

"Easy," he said. "Look."

He pushed his right hand into the opposite sleeve of his blazer. He rummaged for a moment, then there was a crack and the hand emerged holding the lower part of his left arm.

"Cm off," he said, ignoring the brown gunk which dripped from the arm onto his new trousers. The fingers of his left hand wriggled a wave.

It was gross. But it was also impressive and extremely cool. I grinned. Gurr grinned too but when I saw his teeth I stopped smiling. It reminded me of the reason a lot of people were still scared of zombies and I suddenly realised we were standing very close to each other. If he wanted to grab me... if he wanted to bite me... I took a step back.

The Zombie War had been a scary time. I remembered seeing it on the news when I was small and Mum and Dad thought I was too young to understand. A mysterious virus had devastated parts of Europe. It started in Paris and spread, flu-like, through coughs and sneezes. Those who caught it became infected. First came the aching muscles, then the fever, then death. Except it wasn't a normal death. These corpses came back to life, but they were changed. The virus destroyed their brains, rotted their skin and made parts of their bodies fall off. Worst of all, it made them want to eat people. Neighbours had turned on neighbours, friends had murdered friends and parents had devoured their children.

The resurrected creatures had no memories of who they had been, the things they had done, the people they had cared for. They were no longer human. They were zombies, killing machines that roamed the streets, seeking out terrified humans to attack and eat.

In the playground it was a big joke and we chased each other, stumbling, arms outstretched making weird groaning noises. But at night, in the dark, I would get frightened, and sometimes I woke up sweating and shaking from nightmares where I had been chased by real zombies. And they had caught me. And they had torn me apart.

We'd been lucky in Britain where a few small outbreaks had been quickly dealt with. The government spent a lot of money on research and, within three years, scientists had the virus beaten. Some zombies had been captured in the early stages of their infection, and held in camps until the cure was found. They were given the vaccine and all sorts of therapies and treatments to help them remember who they were, and what it was like to be human again. Now, we were told, although those zombies who were released might look scary, they were harmless. Still, looking at Gurr's rough, black teeth I couldn't help wonder. People said some zombies had done horrible things before they were cured.

"When you were... before.... did you ever... eat people?"

Gurr shook his head. I knew he could be lying but I wanted to believe him. And the government said those zombies who were cured had never hurt anyone. They wouldn't lie about a thing like that. Would they?

We walked together in silence until we reached his gate. "Cm," he said, using his dismembered left arm to point at his home.

I stared at the house, and had a strange feeling I was being watched. I imagined Gurr's mum and dad standing in the darkness, eagerly waiting for Gurr to bring home a friend for dinner. The thought made me shudder.

Gurr must have seen my shiver because his mouth twitched in a sad smile. "Morrow?" he asked hopefully.

I thought about what Mum had said that morning. She hadn't told me to stay away from Gurr, just to stay away from the house. And he was in my class. But that was the real problem. My classmates had already shown what they thought of Gurr. If I took his side now, how much of that bullying would be directed at me? For a moment I considered just walking away. Then I thought about whether I wanted idiots like Laura Mosley to dictate who I could talk to. I decided I didn't.

"OK," I said. "Tomorrow. I'll meet you at the bus stop."

Chapter 4

At the bus stop the next morning Gurr and I were reading a poster about a missing dog when Blake showed up. He seemed embarrassed when he saw Gurr and stood a little way off. Eventually he moved closer. He glanced at Gurr, a little guiltily I thought.

"All right?" he mumbled at last.

"O."

"Oh?"

"I think he means OK," I said.

"Ah!"

We stood in silence for a while. Occasionally Blake sneaked a look at Gurr as if to convince himself that he had not suffered permanent damage from the fall the day before. As the bus eventually pulled to a halt in front of us, Blake finally looked Gurr in the face.

"Your head comes off then?"

Gurr nodded.

Blake grinned. "Awesome!"

The three of us took our seats at the back of the bus and, if I'd been super popular the day before, now it was as if Gurr, Blake and I didn't exist. People didn't talk to us or look at us. But that didn't stop them talking about us. Snatches of conversation drifted around the bus. "...zombie best friend," Laura said. "...head came off," Shaun said. "Eye balls." "Disgusting." "Smelly." "Dangerous." It seemed everyone had something to say, and none of it was very nice.

Our first lesson was Maths. I took a seat in the centre of class and pulled a chair out so Gurr could sit next to me. The other kids moved their desks and in seconds we were an island of two. Even Blake sat at the other side of the room. He knew that by befriending Gurr I was making myself unpopular and he wasn't taking any chances.

After sorting her books and writing a few notes, Miss Ward turned to face the class. The friendly smile she normally wore faded when she noticed the space around me and Gurr. She knew exactly what was going on and, unlike yesterday, this teacher wasn't going to ignore it.

"Laura!" she barked. "Move your desk back to its proper place immediately! Isla, Freya, Rokas! Move!"

A series of scraping sounds filled the room as those around us reluctantly dragged desks back to their original positions. Miss Ward waited patiently for silence, all the while staring at the one person who had not moved.

"Laura," she said quietly.

Laura sat, red-faced but determined. "I told my dad about..." she said, her voice quivering. "He said it's not human. It's a monster and it shouldn't be in a class with normal kids."

Miss Ward walked between the desks until she reached Laura then squatted down so they were face to face. "Gary is not a monster," she said, casting a quick glance in our direction. "He is a child who has been the victim of a terrible illness and deserves compassion. So, you can either move your chair back where it belongs or you can spend the rest of the lesson standing in the corridor."

Miss Ward stood up. After a moment's hesitation Laura got off her chair and marched defiantly towards the door. As she passed, she glared at me then at Gurr. "I'll get you for this," she hissed.

I sighed. This meant trouble. Laura was well known for bullying those she thought weaker than her. I could handle it but I was worried for Gurr. I'd have to keep an eye on him. If Laura was going to make his life miserable, he was going to need all the friends he could get.

Chapter 5

"Sausages?"

Gurr shook his head.

"Burgers?"

Gurr shook his head.

"Lamb?"

Gurr shook his head. "Vj," he said.

"Vj?" I repeated.

Gurr pointed to the carrots, peas and broccoli. "Vjit!"

"Vegetables? You want vegetables? No meat?"

"No meat. Vjit!"

I stared at Gurr. After everything I'd heard about what zombies ate (i.e. people), I wasn't prepared for this.

"Are you a vegetarian?" I asked in surprise.

Gurr nodded. "Vjit."

We piled Gurr's plate high with vegetables and looked for a table. I groaned. The only one with places vacant was behind Laura. Even over the buzz of noise in the dining room I could hear her voice.

"... and my dad says they should be sent back to where they came from." She noticed me and glowered.

"And anybody who makes friends with one is an idiot."

As we passed, Gurr stumbled against Laura's table. She shrieked and scrambled backwards.

"Aaagh! It's attacking me! It wants to eat my brains!"

"That would be a very small meal," I said, helping to steady Gurr and move him away. Some of the kids around us smiled.

"Srry," Gurr said. "Fall."

"Uggh! Get it away from me!" Laura demanded. "Get it away!"

I steered Gurr to our table and we sat eating our lunches in silence. Every so often Gurr glanced at Laura as if he was waiting for something. When he caught me looking, he winked.

There was a scream. It was the loudest, shrillest, most piercing scream I'd ever heard. I looked up to see Laura standing by her table, her chair knocked over. Her eyes bulged and her body shook as she stared at the fork in her hand and continued to scream. On the fork was stuck a shrivelled sausage, dripping brown sauce onto the floor. The sausage was wriggling.

The whole room was frozen until Gurr stood up, and calmly walked towards Laura. He reached out and took the sausage.

"Srry," he said. "Fall off." He wiped the goo from the end of his finger, for that is what the sausage was, and popped it back onto his hand.

Laura fainted.

For the next few minutes the dining room was in chaos. Laura Mosley wasn't the most popular student in school and, as people heard that she'd mistaken one of Gurr's fingers for a sausage, there was a rising tide of laughter. Some kids cheered. Others clapped. One or two even gave Gurr a friendly, but tentative, slap on the back. Wiping tears from his eyes, Blake said it was the funniest thing he'd ever seen.

Gurr's shoulders bounced in a series of short spasms and a strange, liquid gurgle rumbled in his throat. I thought for a moment he was choking and then I realised… Gurr was laughing.

Chapter 6

After school we spotted Laura waiting at the bus stop with her friends. She looked angry so I suggested we head through town, catch the number thirty-three, then cut home through the woods to avoid her. Gurr agreed and ten minutes later we were wandering through the precinct towards the bus station.

As we walked, a few people glanced at Gurr. Some scowled but I was glad to see that most either didn't notice or didn't care about the zombie boy walking through the town centre. We entered The Plaza, a busy, wide-open space between stores where people with temporary displays tried to persuade passers-by to change their broadband connection, buy double glazing or sign a petition against whatever they were protesting about that week.

A group of men and women were handing out fliers and attempting to engage bustling shoppers in conversation. Two women pulled a couple of wooden crates together to form a makeshift stage and a squat, fat man stepped onto the crates and held one hand high for silence. He was wearing an old suit made of thick tweed and a bright red bow tie. He had a huge mouth and when he smiled he looked like a horse doing a toothpaste advert. I'd seen the man before at the school gates. It was Laura's dad.

"My friends!" Mr Mosley shouted in a voice that was loud and surprisingly shrill. "I wear this red bow tie today to represent the blood that has been spilt by evil flesh-eating zombies across the world."

A woman passing with her dog paused to listen. A couple of people stopped and murmured their approval.

I touched Gurr's arm. "Come on," I whispered. "We should go." But Gurr didn't move.

"I wear a black armband in memory of all those who were torn apart by the armies of the undead," the shrill voice continued.

I felt increasingly uneasy as some in the growing crowd applauded. I nudged Gurr but he seemed hypnotised by Mr Mosley. If we didn't leave soon it would only be a matter of time before someone noticed us and that wouldn't be good for Gurr. I reached over and pulled his hood up over his head.

"It's happened to our brothers and sisters all over the world, but it will not happen here. We won't let it happen here!"

Two men standing next to the stage unfurled a large banner. It was red with a black square in the middle. In the square, a bolt of lightning was blasting a zombie into pieces. Across the top of the banner were the letters L.A.Z.

"The League Against Zombies will not let it happen here!" Mr Mosley shouted. His arms were raised and both hands were curled into fists.

The crowd cheered. I tugged at Gurr's sleeve and this time he turned.

"We should go."

To my relief Gurr nodded. We shuffled towards the edge of the crowd, which had grown much larger while we were watching the show. Gurr kept his head down so people couldn't see his face.

"They want to allow 'good' zombies to live here," Mr Mosley's voice rang out behind us. "But I say 'no'! What do you say?"

The crowd responded as one. "No!"

"Because the only good zombie..." Mr Mosley said, his voice rising to a terrifying shriek, "...is a dead zombie!"

The crowd laughed and clapped. I gripped Gurr's hand tightly and pulled him through the throng. I was panting and felt sick. There were too many bodies – fat, thin, hard, soft – packed tightly around us. It was getting harder and harder to squeeze past. I began to panic. I took a deep breath.

"Move!"

The shout was as loud as I could make it. For a second I thought it wasn't going to work, but then some of those in front of me turned or edged aside and I saw a flash of daylight. With one final heave I shoved past and the crowd of zombie-haters were behind us. We were free.

I took a deep breath of fresh air and turned to Gurr. But he wasn't there. I was still holding Gurr's hand, but he wasn't on the end of it. He was still in the crowd. This was awful. I couldn't leave him. I saw a gap and started to push back through the bodies.

"Nthn!"

I turned to see Gurr emerging a few feet away. Quickly I pulled back and ran to him. He took his hand and pushed it back onto his wrist. Together we started to hurry away, but were forced to stop when a familiar figure stepped in front of us. She wore a wide smile and her eyes gleamed in triumph. She pointed directly at Gurr.

"Look!" Laura shrieked. "It's an evil, flesh-eating zombie!"

The crowd turned. I grabbed Gurr's arm.

"Run!"

Chapter 7

I was captain of the school rugby team and knew I could outrun a group of middle-aged shoppers without any trouble. But Gurr couldn't. He was gangly and ungainly and ran as if his legs belonged to someone else. His left leg swung in a wide arc, while his right leg seemed to half hop and half stumble in the general direction of where he wanted to go. Watching Gurr trying to run was like watching a giraffe trying to ice-skate.

At first most people seemed content to shout rude words after us. We heard lots of whistles and boos but there was no real threat until Mr Mosley and Laura pushed their way to the front.

"Go back to where you came from," he yelled.

"Monster!" shouted someone.

"Murderer!"

"We don't want something like that in our town, do we?" Mr Mosley appealed to the crowd.

A small group edged forward murmuring their agreement. "No!"

"We're not going to let it escape are we?"

"No!"

"Then let's get it!"

Mr Mosley broke into a run. Laura ran after him, and soon we were being pursued by a horde of screaming vigilantes.

We had a start on them but with Gurr's unique running style it wasn't going to be long before they caught us. I looked around frantically, hoping to see a police officer or someone willing to help, but it seemed no one was interested in two children being chased by a baying mob. So if no one was going to help and we couldn't run away, we only had one option left. We had to hide.

"Down here!" I said, pulling Gurr around a corner towards a narrow alley that I knew ran between two shops. It was one of those places you could pass every day and not notice unless you were looking for it. With luck we could hide in the alley until the mob passed, and then head the other way to the bus station. I was just congratulating myself on a genius plan when one of Gurr's feet flew off. Gurr stumbled, grabbed hold of me and we crashed to the ground. Before we could get up I heard a shout.

"There they are!"

The mob rounded the corner and quickly encircled us. Some looked confused, like a dog that had chased a car, caught it and then didn't know what to do with it. But a couple of them looked wild and threatening. Laura looked on, grinning, as Mr Mosley glared down at me.

"Traitor!" he hissed, in his thin, reedy voice. "You'd better get out of here while you can. It's him we want."

He grabbed Gurr roughly by his shirt, dragging him upwards. Gurr gave a frightened yelp.

"Let him go!" I yelled, jumping to my feet, but I was instantly seized from behind.

"I've heard that bits of you drop off," Mr Mosley said, pinching Gurr's ear between his finger and thumb. "Maybe I'll feed this to my dog." He pulled and Gurr's ear came away with a sickly ripping sound.

Gurr roared in frustration and anger, and a couple of people laughed, but most seemed scared and uneasy at the assault.

"Leave him alone!" I shouted, struggling to get away from the strong hands that held me firmly.

"You'd better shut your mouth," Mr Mosley snapped. "Or the next ear I pull off will be yours."

A grey hand reached through the small crowd and plucked the ear from Mr Mosley's fingers.

"Thank," a gravelly voice said.

Someone screamed. I felt the grip on my arms weaken and I pulled myself free. The crowd parted to reveal two strange figures. From their appearance, and Gurr's sigh of relief, it was obvious who they were.

Gurr's dad was short and painfully skinny. His black trousers flapped as if there were no legs inside them, and his white shirt hung limply from coat hanger-like shoulders. His face was the colour of clay and part of his cheek was missing, giving him a permanent snarl that reminded me of an angry wolf. On his head sat an ill-fitting wig which had slipped to one side revealing raw, pink patches of skin and tufts of brittle hair. He glared at the crowd with wild, staring eyes and growled menacingly.

Gurr's mum was even scarier. She was bald and her face was taut and skull-like with sunken eyes. There were two holes where her nose should be. She stood almost six feet tall and the long, shapeless dress which came down to her feet, made her appear even taller. The dress was sleeveless, revealing a pair of knobbly shoulders and skeletal arms ending in withered hands and bony fingers. She barked, like an angry puppy. In one hand she held Gurr's ear.

The mob, who moments before had been bravely threatening two children, now froze. It seemed their courage didn't extend to taking on two adult zombies. For a couple of seconds no one moved, then Gurr's mum seemed to float forward, her bare arms outstretched.

"Eeeeat! Braaains!"

Mr Mosley shrieked, staggered backwards, tripped over someone's foot and fell to the ground. That was the signal for everyone else to panic. They turned and ran, pushing and shoving to get away as fast as they could. Leaving her dad on the ground, Laura ran with them. Gibbering, Mr Mosley scrambled to his feet and sprinted after the others, constantly glancing back over his shoulder until he ran into a wall, staggered then disappeared around a corner. As quickly as that, the mob was gone.

I was about to celebrate when Gurr's mum turned and put her hands on my shoulders, her bony fingers digging into my skin. I tried to pull away but her grip was too strong. Her face loomed over me, and I could see her jagged teeth as her jaws opened. I wanted to scream but I couldn't. Her mouth came towards my face and I breathed in her rancid breath as she pulled me closer and... kissed my cheek.

"Thank," she said and smiled.

She stuck Gurr's ear back on his head and pulled him close for a hug. I would never have thought that a zombie's eyes could twinkle mischievously, but hers did. "No. Eat. Brains," she said "Joke." And she gurgled a noise which could only have been laughter.

Mr Agger didn't laugh. His forehead furrowed and he grunted unhappily as he rescued Gurr's foot from the mouth of a passing bulldog. "Trble," he said. "Bad trble cming."

Chapter 8

Mr and Mrs Agger drove us home in their car. It was a battered old thing that creaked and banged over the uneven roads. Mr Agger drove with a permanent frown of concentration, as if afraid he'd forget how to do it at any moment. Every time he changed gear there was a painful grinding of metal.

Mrs Agger noted my concern. "Just. Passed. Test," she said, yelping a quiet bark. She nudged her husband playfully. "Doing. Good."

Mr Agger grunted, never shifting his gaze from the road ahead.

"Music?" Mrs Agger asked.

Gurr shook his head frantically. "No!"

Mrs Agger ignored him and slid a CD into the player. The cheery tinkle of a piano filled the car and a woman I recognised from kids' TV started to sing a nursery rhyme. Mrs Agger joined in. Her voice was deep and crackly.

"Happy. Know it. Hands. Happy. Know it. Hands. Happy. Know it. Show it. Happy. Know it. Hands."

She accompanied herself by doing all the movements, clapping her hands, stamping her feet and nodding her head. I looked at Gurr who was sitting with his eyes closed, wishing he was anywhere but here.

Mrs Agger glanced over her bony shoulder. "All. Parents. Embarrass," she said and gurgled her strange laugh. "Come. Join. In."

I bit my lip then caught Gurr looking at me. I snorted. The ends of his lips curled upwards. By the time we reached our street we were giggling helplessly and trying to join in with 'Incy Wincy Spider' like a couple of five year olds.

Mum was in the garden when the car pulled up and I jumped out.

"Nathan! What are you ...?" Mum began, then stopped as Mr and Mrs Agger got out of the car. Her eyes widened and her mouth dropped open in surprise. This was the first time she had seen our new neighbours properly and she was clearly shaken.

"We were attacked," I said, before she could say anything more. "Mr and Mrs Agger saved us."

Mum closed her mouth, and gave the Aggers a wary nod of thanks. They smiled in return. It was meant to be friendly, but the sight of all those teeth made Mum swallow and take a step back. She watched them go, the relief evident on her face.

"We'll talk about this later," she said. "But right now we've got something more important to worry about. It's Buzby. He's missing."

Chapter 9

Mum told me she'd let Buzby into the garden after breakfast, as she did every day, but when she came out later he was gone. She slid an arm around my shoulder. "I'm sure he'll be back. He can't have gone far."

My heart dropped into my stomach. I felt sick. "Did you look for him?"

"Of course I did. I've been walking the streets all day."

"But he never leaves the garden without us! Never!"

Mum forced a smile. "As soon as he gets hungry he'll come trotting up the path. You'll see." She turned back to the house. "Dinner's nearly ready. Ten minutes." Her face hardened. "Then we can talk about your new friends."

I didn't follow Mum. I couldn't think about dinner. All I could think about was Buzby. He wasn't used to being out on his own. I thought about all the dangers that were out there – fast cars, deep rivers, fierce dogs and a hundred other things that could hurt him.

Buzby was already five years old and lame when I picked him out at the rescue centre. Dad had steered me towards an excitable Labrador puppy that hopped and danced as we approached, and Buzby was in the next pound. He didn't skip or bark to attract attention. He just stood with his snout sticking through the mesh of his cage. When he spotted me looking he turned away, as if offended, and limped over to his food bowl.

"Him," I said.

"Really?" my Dad replied, frowning. "He's a bit boring, Nathan. Wouldn't you rather…?"

I shook my head. The puppy was cute and furry with huge brown eyes and exactly the kind of dog I should've wanted, but he just didn't interest me. I still don't know why. Maybe it was because Buzby looked so sad and I wanted to help. It's hard to recall exactly what I felt back then but I do remember one thing clearly. I'd made up my mind I was having Buzby, and I wasn't going to be swayed.

"I want him."

"There are more dogs down…"

"I want this one!"

It was my sixth birthday so Dad shrugged, paid the fee, and I became the new owner of a greying, occasionally bad-tempered Yorkshire Terrier with a gammy leg. And I loved him.

I noticed Gurr standing in his garden. "Buzby's gone. I have to find him," I said, walking towards him.

Gurr frowned.

"My dog," I explained. "I've had Buzby since I was little. He never goes off on his own."

"Hlp. Like dgs."

I wasn't in the mood for talking and Gurr seemed OK with that, so we trudged around the estate in silence. We didn't see any sign of Buzby but we did see posters for other missing animals – dogs, cats, rabbits, guinea pigs. It seemed like every pet on the estate had gone missing.

Eventually it started getting dark. Mum would be worried. I led Gurr off the path. If we walked back the way we came it would take half an hour, but cutting through the Jungle would bring us back to our street in just a few minutes.

The Jungle was the local name for an area of woodland in the middle of our horseshoe-shaped estate. Mum didn't like me going there. There were some boggy areas that were dangerous but it was pretty safe if you knew what you were doing, and I did. I'd played there with friends more times than I could remember. Games of pirates and spacemen and monsters. We'd run all over the Jungle and I knew every inch.

"Zombie freaks. We'll sort 'em out."

I recognised the high-pitched voice immediately and for a moment thought the comment was aimed at us. I saw movement through the trees. It was Mr Mosley and he was coming our way.

"Quick, down here!" I whispered. I led Gurr down a hidden dirt track and dropped to my knees. "Follow me."

I crawled through a thicket and emerged into a natural den with walls and a roof made up of leaves and twisted branches. It was a hiding place I used when I wanted to be on my own. I sometimes brought Buzby when I took him for a walk and the thought made me sad. Buzby had to be OK. He just had to be. Gurr followed me into the den and we sat, hardly daring to breathe.

"My house is starting to stink," a man's voice muttered. "We need to sort it."

"We will," Mr Mosley replied. "Don't worry. I'll get you some help."

The voices faded as the men passed and walked further into the woods. Gurr and I waited a few minutes, and then slipped out of the den and headed back to the estate. We separated at Gurr's garden gate and I was about to thank him for coming with me when I noticed the graffiti. Someone had spray-painted a lightning flash and the words 'Go Home' in large, red letters on the side of his house.

The League Against Zombies had paid the Aggers a visit.

Chapter 10

Dad was more relaxed than Mum about zombies living next door and I think they must have talked because she was far less angry than I thought she'd be when I got home. And when I explained what had happened in town and about the graffiti, she seemed almost sorry for the Aggers. So she didn't ban me from seeing Gurr, but she still said I was never to go into their house.

At school next day Gurr and Laura avoided each other, although I did notice Laura give him some evil stares. If Laura's eyes had been lasers, Gurr would have been burnt to a crisp.

The 'sausage finger' incident was still being talked about and partly because people thought it was funny, but mostly because so many disliked Laura, Gurr was suddenly treated much better. In class no one moved their desks away. In Maths (which Gurr turned out to be brilliant at) Denell asked for his help on an algebra question. And in Science when Gurr accidentally knocked his books onto the floor, Shaun helped to pick them up.

Things were going so well that when I had to leave Gurr at lunchtime I was pretty confident he'd be all right, especially as Blake and Patreece both said they'd look out for him and keep him out of Laura's way.

I had to go to the gym because on Sunday we were playing in the final of the Schools Rugby Cup and, as I was captain, Mr Davies wanted to give me the final arrangements and talk through tactics. I was on my way back to find the others when I heard shouts and saw people running. Instinctively, I knew Gurr was in trouble.

I ran after the crowd and pushed my way through into the science lab. Gurr was standing in the middle of the room, clutching the school's pet rabbit to his chest. He looked terrified.

Mr Webster entered and glared at Gurr. "What are you doing with Daisy Flopsy Ears?" he demanded.

Gurr looked at Mr Webster, then at the rabbit, then back at Mr Webster. He pulled Daisy closer.

"Eat."

Chapter 11

There were cries of horror from the children.

"He wants to eat Daisy Flopsy Ears!" someone squealed over the noise. It was Laura. She pointed at Gurr and was doing her best to look scared and horrified, but I also saw her give the briefest of smiles.

Gurr's bottom lip trembled as he surveyed the hostile faces around him. He spotted me and took a hopeful step forward, offering me the rabbit.

"Don't…" he began, but stopped as Laura pushed in front of him.

"I'll save you!" Laura snatched the rabbit from Gurr's hands and ran with it to the far corner of the room where she stood stroking Daisy's thick white fur. "It's all right Daisy," she crooned. "I won't let the nasty freak eat you."

"Right! Everybody out!" Mr Webster shouted. "Go on! Get to your next class! Now!" His voice softened. "You can put Daisy back in her cage, Laura. I think she's safe now."

Reluctantly the crowd began to break up. Gurr stood, shaking and confused as they passed, some of them muttering insults and threats. Among them were many of the new friends he'd made that morning. Laura was last to leave, preening as her new group of admirers told her how brave she was.

Mr Webster noticed me loitering. "Go on Nathan. Get to your class."

"But Gurr wouldn't eat a rabbit," I said. "He's vegetarian."

"I'm sure all zombies are vegetarians until they eat somebody," Mr Webster sneered. "You heard him. Eat, he said!"

I wanted to defend Gurr but, much as I hated to admit it, Mr Webster was right. Gurr had been caught holding the school pet, and in front of a dozen witnesses had said he wanted to eat it.

"What were you doing Gurr?" I asked.

"Eat." His voice sounded desperate.

Mr Webster wore a thin smile as he looked Gurr up and down in obvious disgust. "I told them it was a mistake. Things like you don't belong in a normal school. And with a bit of luck you won't be here much longer." He flicked a hand in Gurr's direction. "Out," he said.

As they left, something orange dropped from Gurr's hand and rolled away. I picked it up. That's odd, I thought. Why was Gurr holding a carrot?

I stared at the vegetable for a long time, puzzled. Then suddenly I understood. When Gurr said 'Eat' he wasn't talking about himself. He was talking about Daisy. Gurr wasn't going to eat the rabbit. He was going to feed the rabbit. And once I understood that, something else became clear. It wasn't an accident that Laura had been here to find Gurr with Daisy and raise the alarm. It was deliberate. Gurr had been set up.

Chapter 12

Art was our next lesson but it didn't start for another five minutes. I ran to the art room hoping Blake and Patreece would be there. They were.

"You were supposed to watch him," I shouted. "What were you doing?"

Patreece shrugged. "It's not my fault he wanted a bunny burger," he said. "You told us he was veggie."

"Why did you let him go to the lab?"

"He was sent for," Blake said. "We reckoned he'd be safe enough with a teacher."

"Which teacher?"

"I don't know. He got a note."

"Where is it?"

"I don't know."

"Maybe he ate it," Patreece said. "Seems he eats everything else."

It took another two minutes of questioning before Blake remembered that Gurr might have dropped the note in the bin next to the bike sheds, or it could have been the bin near the fire doors, or maybe even the bin by the changing rooms. I sprinted away while they were still talking.

"Where you going?" Blake called after me. I didn't answer.

I ran down the corridor and burst through the doors into the quad. I was convinced the note had come from Laura and I needed to prove it. I reached the first bin and tipped it onto the floor. Empty cola cans, pop bottles, crisp packets and old food tumbled around my feet. I scrabbled through the rubbish searching for anything that looked like a note. There was nothing.

I ran to the second bin and tipped it up. Someone had emptied a bottle of water into the bin and all of the rubbish was wet and stank. I picked through it carefully. The note was not there.

I was searching the contents of the third bin when I heard an angry voice behind me.

"Oi! What do you think you're doing?" It was Mr Dempsey, the caretaker.

Mr Dempsey was a short, thin man with a bald head and red, bulbous nose. His nickname was Rudolph, but we would never call him that to his face. His was not a face you could have a joke with. His was a face you wanted as a mask at Halloween to scare the neighbours. There was a legend that Mr Dempsey had once smiled at a child but no one really believed it. But if it had happened I was sure that child would have had nightmares for weeks afterwards.

"I'm sorry…" I said.

"Aye! Sorry you got caught. Do you think I keep this place clean for fun?"

"No, I…"

"Do you think I sweep this yard every day for the pure joy of it?"

"No, but…"

"Do you think I drive into work praying that some thoughtful little monster will give up their valuable time to fill this quad with tons of stinking litter, just so I can experience the sheer delight and overwhelming bliss that comes from sweeping it all back up again?"

"I was looking for a note," I managed to stammer.

"Oh, a note!" Mr Dempsey said. "I didn't realise you were looking for a note. You didn't say you were looking for a note. If I'd known you were looking for a note I would've got down on my poor, arthritic knees and sorted through this putrid pile of garbage until we found it."

I was amazed. "Would you really?"

Mr Dempsey stared at me like I had crawled from under a stone and then been sick on his shoes. "No!" he said. "Come with me. Head's office. Now."

I groaned. By trying to get Gurr out of trouble, it seemed all I'd done was get myself into it.

Chapter 13

Reluctantly I followed Mr Dempsey and my foot kicked a piece of paper. It lifted in the light wind and as it floated away I saw a single word – Gurr.

"There it is!" I shouted and ran after the note.

"Oi! Come back 'ere!" Mr Dempsey yelled and set off after me.

The wind blew the paper across the yard. Every time I tried to catch it or stamp on it, the breeze lifted it away. I ran the whole length of the quad, right up to the school doors. The wind strengthened and blew the note high into the sky and for a moment it was gone. Then the wind dropped and it slowly fluttered to the ground in front of me. I picked up the note and was still reading it when Mr Dempsey arrived, out of breath.

"I have never..." he began, then stopped when the door opened and Mr Webster stepped out.

"What are you doing out of class?" he said.

"Throwing rubbish about, that's what he's doing," Mr Dempsey gasped between breaths. He indicated the litter-strewn quad behind us.

"Did you do that?" Mr Webster asked.

"Yes, but..."

"Hooligan!" Mr Dempsey said. "I spend hours keeping this place clean and does anybody care? I have enough to do without young vandals..."

"Thank you, Mr Dempsey," Mr Webster said. "I'll deal with him."

"Aye, well, make sure you do," the caretaker grumbled. "And he can clean it up, 'cos I'm not." And he gave me a dark look before walking away mumbling to himself.

Mr Webster turned his attention to me and frowned. "Explain," he said.

I took a deep breath. "Did you send a note to Gurr telling him to go to the lab?" I asked, pushing the piece of paper into his hand. I knew Mr Webster disliked Gurr but he was a teacher and he had to be fair. And when he saw the note was in Laura's handwriting he'd have no choice but to do something about it.

Mr Webster scanned the note and read it aloud. "Gurr, come to the science lab immediately. Mr Webster."

"You didn't send it, did you sir?"

Mr Webster seemed to consider the question for a moment. "Yes," he said at last. "I sent it."

"But..." I stammered. I could barely speak. Mr Webster was lying and we both knew it.

"If this is meant as a defence of your friend's actions you need to read the note again. It says 'come to the science lab'. It does not say 'come to the science lab and eat the school's pet rabbit'."

"But Laura Mosley set him up!" I said. "She wrote that note. You know she did."

Even as I said the words I could hardly believe it was me speaking. I was accusing a teacher of lying! My blood seemed to freeze in my veins as I waited for Mr Webster to explode.

Without taking his gaze from mine Mr Webster slowly, and very deliberately, tore the note into small pieces and put them in his pocket. He bent slightly until his face was just inches from mine. "If you think I didn't write the note, prove it," he whispered softly. "And if you can't prove it, I suggest you keep your mouth shut. A child who makes false accusations against a teacher could find themselves in very, very serious trouble."

I didn't know what to say. I couldn't believe what was happening. But I also knew he was right. He had the note and I couldn't prove anything. Who would believe me over a teacher?

"Now, clear up this mess and later you can join me for detention," Mr Webster said. He turned and walked towards the school. As he reached the door he stopped and looked back. He was wearing a broad smile. "And don't worry about the zombie," he said. "He's already been suspended."

By the time I finished detention and got home, Mum already knew about Gurr's suspension. And in the version she'd heard, Gurr had actually been caught eating the rabbit.

"But it's not true," I said. "That's not what happened."

"I knew it," Mum continued, ignoring me and peering across at the Aggers' house. "I said it when they moved in and I was right. They're dangerous and the sooner they clear out the better."

I knew there was no point arguing. Once Mum got an idea into her head it was very hard to shift it. I went up to my room and sat on the bed. Outside I could see Gurr in his garden. He was on a swing but he wasn't swinging. He was just sitting, staring at the ground. I went over and knocked on the window and waved, but he either didn't see me or didn't care because he didn't wave back.

Chapter 14

The next morning was Saturday and, as I ate my breakfast, Dad sat on the settee reading the local newspaper. Every so often he'd sigh and shake his head. Eventually he stood up and dropped the newspaper onto the table next to me.

"You should read this," he said.

I looked at Dad in surprise. I never read the newspaper. Dad just raised his eyebrows, sat back in his chair and drank his mug of tea. Curious I turned to the front page and read the main story.

Zombies attack peaceful protest

A peaceful demonstration turned into a day of terror earlier this week when zombies attacked a small group of protestors. One witness who did not want to be named for fear of reprisals said, "We left the demo' to get a coffee when suddenly two huge, slavering zombies appeared from nowhere. They grabbed at us, trying to bite us. One was screaming that she'd eat our brains. We managed to fight them off and escape but it was terrifying. Something should be done."

Mr Gavin Mosley, leader of the respected organisation League

Against Zombies, added, "This was a lawful protest calling on the council to put more safeguards in place to protect residents from these creatures. Yesterday's attack proves they are dangerous and must be stopped."

"But they attacked us!" I said. "Mr Mosley pulled Gurr's ear off! Why isn't that in the 'paper?"

Dad shrugged. "Newspapers don't always print the full truth, son, or even most of it. Sometimes they just print what people want to read."

"The Aggers could've attacked Mr Mosley but they didn't. They just scared him off. And they might look weird but that shouldn't matter. They're nice and Mrs Agger's really funny."

Dad came over and sat on the chair next to mine. "The Aggers are different, Nathan," he said, placing his mug on the table. "People are sometimes scared of those who are different. Especially when they've been known to bite people's faces off."

"But the Aggers are not like that."

"Maybe not," Dad said. "But some people still need convincing. And stories like these won't help."

He turned the page and pointed to a black and white photograph at the top. It was of a young girl, looking very pleased with herself. In her arms she was cuddling a white rabbit. I groaned as I read the story.

Boy suspended after rabbit attack
A boy was suspended from a local school yesterday after trying to eat the school's pet rabbit. One witness, 11 year old Laura Mosley said, "It was horrible. He was spitting and snarling. His long finger nails were tearing at Daisy Flopsy Ears' fur. I managed to get the rabbit away from him but it was terrifying. Things like that shouldn't be in our school. They're dangerous."

Due to his age the boy cannot be named, but it is understood that police believe there may be a link between this incident and the growing number of missing pets in the area.

A spokesman for the police said, "We can confirm that dozens of residents have reported lost animals this week. We do not know what has caused this situation, but we are investigating (See Comment)."

With a sinking feeling in my stomach, I turned to the Editor's comments column.

Comment

In the space of just a few days, zombie attacks and missing pets have brought terror and anguish to the law-abiding residents of Evans City. This newspaper asks the police to consider if it is a coincidence that people have been assaulted and pets have disappeared immediately after a certain family moved into the area.

This newspaper is not saying the family are sneaking through our streets at night, stealing pets and eating them, but do we have any evidence that they are not? And, if they are, where will it end? What will they do if they are confronted? What will they eat when they run out of pets? Are we safe? Are our children safe? This newspaper demands that the police act now.

"But this is all wrong," I said. "They're making it look like Gurr and his family are violent and dangerous. It's not fair!"

"Life's not fair," Dad said. "The sooner you learn that, the better." He rested a hand on my shoulder and gave it a little squeeze. "Look Nathan, the Aggers could be innocent, but you can't be sure. How much do we really know about them, eh?"

I jumped to my feet, furious that Dad would even consider there could be some truth in the stories. "I know they're vegetarians. I know they don't attack people."

Dad shook his head. "Me and your mum have been talking, and your safety's the most important thing in the world to us. So from now on, you stay away from them. All of them."

"But Gurr's my friend," I said.

"Not any more."

I stared at Dad in disbelief. "So I've got to dump Gurr, just 'cos he's different and the newspaper tells lies about him?"

"For now," Dad said. "Once it's all sorted…" He looked embarrassed, maybe even ashamed.

"Well, I won't!" I shouted. "And you can't make me!"

Angrily, I swept the newspaper off the table and stormed out of the kitchen. Dad called after me but I ignored him as I ran out of the house and slammed the front door behind me. I didn't care what Mum and Dad thought. I didn't care what the newspapers said. Gurr was my friend and I was going to help him.

I just didn't know how.

Chapter 15

I'd barely reached the gate when four police cars and two vans roared into the street, sirens blaring. They screeched to a halt outside the Aggers' house and at least a dozen police officers leapt out. They ran into the garden, some covering the front of the house while others went around the back.

I raced towards the house as one broad-shouldered officer strode up the path and beat his fist on the door. There was a pause, and then the door opened. Mr Agger appeared in the doorway. When he saw the uniformed man at his door and the police in his garden, his shoulders slumped. He'd said there would be bad trouble and here it was.

The officer held up an identification badge. "Mr Agger? My name is Inspector McKeown," he said pleasantly. "I wonder if you and your wife would accompany me to the police station. Some accusations have been made regarding an attack in the town centre and we'd like to ask you a few questions."

Mr Agger shook his head. "Attck my boy," he said. "Dfnd him."

"That's true," I shouted, running into the garden. "I was there. They attacked us. All Mr and Mrs Agger did was scare them off."

The inspector turned to me and raised one eyebrow. "And you are?"

"Nathan." I pointed to my house. "I live there."

"Well, thank you for that, Nathan. I'll send someone to get your statement later."

The inspector turned his attention back to Mr Agger. Gurr and Mrs Agger had joined him at the door. She was wearing a t-shirt that said 'We're zombies! Get used to it!'

"If you could come with me and answer a few questions, I'm sure you'll be back before you know it."

Reluctantly, Mr Agger nodded. Mrs Agger barked and placed an arm protectively around Gurr's shoulder.

"Ah, yes! The boy," the inspector murmured. "Do you have any friends who can look after him until you come back?"

Mrs Agger looked at me and I looked at Mum and Dad who were now standing in our doorway.

"Mum?"

Mum shook her head.

Mrs Agger turned to the inspector. "No," she said sadly. "No. Friends."

"Then the child can come too. I'm sure we'll find something to keep him occupied." The inspector waved a hand towards the vehicles in the road. "I don't think we'll need the vans today. We'll travel to the station in the cars. Let's keep it informal, eh?"

Mr Agger stepped out of the house. Mrs Agger and Gurr followed, closing the door behind them. They walked past me and the police closed in around them. Across the street I saw a neighbour's curtain twitch. Others had come out to watch the show, no doubt hoping the police would drag away the unwelcome newcomers.

"It'll be OK!" I called. "I'll tell them the truth!"

The Aggers were almost at the cars when a tall, skinny sergeant came from around the back of the house and caught up with the inspector. He was carrying a black bin bag. "This was in the shed, sir," he said.

The sergeant pulled out a handful of leather and plastic bands, dropping some as he did so. They were a variety of colours and sizes, with tags hanging off them. They were all different, but they were all the same thing. They were dog and cat collars.

The inspector examined the collars and nodded to himself. With a deep sigh he turned to Gurr's parents who were both frantically shaking their heads.

"Not. Ours."

"Never. Seen. Bag."

While some of the police grinned like they had just won the lottery, the inspector looked almost disappointed.

"Mr and Mrs Agger, I'm arresting you on a charge of theft. You do not have to say anything…"

The rest of the inspector's words faded to a blur as a bright red collar on the ground caught my eye. I grabbed it before anyone could stop me and read the attached tag.

'Buzby'.

I stood frozen, gripping Buzby's collar and thinking about the article in that morning's newspaper. Was it true? Were the Aggers stealing pets to eat? And what had Gurr said the night before? That he liked dogs. What if he meant…? My face was hot with anger and I felt tears welling up in my eyes.

I pushed past the inspector to stand in front of Gurr, my nose almost touching his.

"Did you take Buzby?" I hissed. "Did you eat my dog?"

Gurr took a step backwards. "No!" he stammered. "No! Wdn't! Vj!" He looked around frantically and his mum and dad moved closer to protect him. At that moment I hated them all.

The sergeant moved me aside and I watched, angry and miserable, as the police helped the Agger family into the cars. I'd thought Gurr was my friend but I'd been an idiot. Everyone had tried to warn me but I'd ignored them, and now Buzby was gone and it was my fault. Mum and Dad were right. The newspaper was right. Mr Webster was right. It would be better if Gurr and his zombie parents left and never came back.

Chapter 16

After giving my statement to the police, I searched the Jungle but there was no sign of Buzby. The more I thought about it, the more I was convinced something horrible had happened to him. Something horrible that involved Gurr and his parents.

When I got home Mum gave me a hug and made me some dinner, but didn't ask where I'd been. She knows when I'm upset I want quiet and to be on my own. So I ate my dinner and went to my room. I lay on the bed thinking about Buzby. Buzby growling at the fire because it was too hot, but refusing to move from his favourite spot. Buzby savaging my shoes while I was still wearing them. Buzby licking my face and trying to stick his tongue up my nose. It hurt to think about him but it also made me feel better. I cried for a while and that made me feel better too. A bit.

I hung Buzby's collar on the end of my bed and lay there just looking at it. I must have fallen asleep because the next thing I knew it was dark and the house was silent. The display on the clock by my bed showed 11:30. I stood up and stretched. It felt strange to be awake when everyone else was asleep. I wandered over to the window and thought back just a few days to when I'd watched the new family moving in next door. I was excited then, but now I wished I'd never set eyes on our new neighbours.

Through the glass, the bright moonlight cast a strange silver glow which made my skin appear pale and lifeless, like a fish on a slab. Or like a zombie. The thought made me shiver. I stared at Gurr's house.

I was about to turn away when something in the garden caught my eye. I pressed my nose against the window and cupped my face with my hands. Everything was still. Then there was movement. A shadow by the house. The front door opened and a figure slipped inside. The door closed and the figure was gone. But not before I'd recognised him. It was Gurr. My stomach lurched as I realised what I had to do. A moment ago I'd never wanted to see Gurr again, but now I knew I had to talk to him. I had to find out the truth.

Avoiding the creaking floor-board on the landing, I sneaked downstairs as quietly as I could. The front door key was in a bowl on a stand. It was on a fob with the key for Dad's car and a couple of keys he used at work. I picked up the fob and as I turned it slipped through my fingers. The collection of keys hit the hardwood floor with a crack which seemed abnormally loud in the otherwise silent night. I froze. Mum and Dad were bound to have heard it.

I stood for a long time, barely breathing, feeling my heart thump in my chest. Gradually, I began to relax. There was no noise, no movement from upstairs. I let out the breath I had been holding and picked up the keys. Holding them tightly I unlocked the door, flinching at the click as the lock turned. I opened the door and, pausing only to slip on my trainers, I stepped outside and closed the door behind me.

The cold hit me immediately but I was not going back for a coat. I ran to Gurr's house. I didn't knock. I just turned the handle and pushed the door inwards. It opened with a faint creak and I stepped inside.

I paused, suddenly aware of what I was doing. I'd seen Gurr, but what if they'd all escaped from the police? What if they'd all come back? Zombies ate people, and I was about to enter their house. What if they were in there now, waiting? My mouth went dry and I had a sudden urge to run home, lock the door and hide under my duvet.

A low, whimpering moan came from somewhere close by. It didn't sound like anything that was likely to tear my intestines out and have them for supper. It sounded... pathetic. I took a deep breath and walked into the lounge. Gurr was sitting on the floor with a book in his lap and a small torch in his hand. He glanced up when I entered but didn't seem surprised to see me. He just turned his attention back to the book. In the light of the torch, I could see glistening lines on his cheeks where he'd been crying.

Looking at Gurr, I suddenly realised I didn't know what to do or what to say, so I just sat next to him. Closer now I could see that the book was a photograph album, filled with pictures of a young couple. A tall woman with an impish grin, the man shorter with a cheerful, open face. In some of the photographs they were holding a small child with wild hair and plump red cheeks. In all of the photographs the family was smiling or laughing. They looked happy. They looked normal.

It was odd. Looking at the Aggers, I'd never considered what they were like before the virus. I'd just thought of them as zombies. But looking at the pictures I could see that once they'd been a mum, a dad and a child. They'd been an ordinary family. An ordinary family just like mine. It made me wonder what would've happened to us if we'd been infected. Would people have been scared of us? Would they have hated us? Would we have changed into monsters or would we have held on to who we were?

"Did you take the pets?" I asked quietly.

Gurr didn't reply. Instead he turned the pages of the album until he reached a photograph which he tapped with his finger. It showed Gurr, as a toddler, posing proudly with his parents outside a small shop. In the window a large poster told the world that it was 'Opening Today'. A professionally painted sign above the window read 'Aggers' Vegetarian and Vegan Foods'.

"Vj!" Gurr insisted, drumming his finger on the page. "Vj!"

I nodded and I understood. The Aggers had not stolen the pets. They had not stolen Buzby. They had been set up, just as Laura had set up Gurr with the rabbit. And I had a good idea of who had done it. It was the League Against Zombies who had sprayed graffiti on the Aggers' house the night before and it was Mr Mosley and one of his cronies we'd hidden from in the woods. What else had they done during their visit? Had they planted a bag full of pet collars and tipped-off the police where to find them?

I opened my mouth to speak but before I could tell Gurr I believed him, a light flashed bright blue across the walls. The police had arrived. And they'd come for Gurr.

Chapter 17

Gurr stood up, put the album onto a shelf and walked to the door. I stepped in front of him, barring his way. "You have to hide!" I said.

Gurr glanced out of the window and I followed his gaze. Three police cars were parked erratically on the road, their blue lights strobing, and a group of dark figures were heading for the house. Gurr placed a gnarled hand on my shoulder. "Nt eat Bzby! Nvr!"

"I know. I'm sorry," I said. "You and your parents wouldn't do that. You're vj, right?"

Gurr nodded. "Vj."

We heard the front door open and the sound of heavy footsteps in the hallway. A moment later the room was filled with people in uniform. "Grab him!" someone shouted, but nobody moved. It seemed even the police were wary of zombies.

"Nobody's grabbing anybody," a voice said firmly, and a large figure shouldered his way to the front. It was the inspector who had arrested Gurr's parents earlier.

"You had me worried, lad," he said, bending so his head was level with Gurr's. "There are some nasty folk in this town who don't like you and your family. It's really not safe for you to be out on your own."

"He wasn't on his own," I said. "I was with him."

Noticing me for the first time, the inspector straightened. "Helped him escape did you?" he asked with a frown. "You do know that harbouring a criminal can put you in prison for ten years?"

"But... I... no..." I stammered.

The inspector's sombre face broke into a smile. "Just my little joke," he said, chuckling. "It's good that Gurr's got a friend. But you lad, you need to come back with me." He gently took hold of Gurr's arm and guided him out of the house.

I pushed my way through the throng of police and caught up with them in the garden. "But you can't put him in prison," I shouted. "He hasn't done anything wrong. It's not fair."

"Prison?" the inspector said, turning to face me. "Gurr wasn't in prison, lad. He was staying with me. We thought he was in bed until we popped in to say goodnight, and found he'd gone."

"You let him stay with you?" The voice was Dad's. He and Mum had come out to see what the fuss was about and were standing by the fence in their dressing gowns. If they were surprised to see me in the garden at that time of night, they didn't show it.

"Why not?" the inspector said. "You're not dangerous are you, lad?"

"But you arrested them," Mum insisted.

"There was a complaint which we have to investigate. But ask yourself this. Do you really think the council would put flesh-eating zombies in the middle of the estate?" The inspector shook his head. "Mr and Mrs Agger were thoroughly checked before they were allowed to come here. The virus didn't completely turn them. They were all vegetarians before they were infected and they're all vegetarians now. They're not dangerous. Their only crime is being different."

"But what about our Buzby and the missing pets? What about the collars?" Dad said.

"They were put there to get the Aggers into trouble," I cut in. "They didn't take Buzby. I'm sure of it."

"I can't comment on that right now," the inspector said. "But maybe you should listen to your son." He placed a hand on Gurr's back. "Come on lad, let's get you back home."

I walked with them to the car and stood back as the inspector opened the rear door for Gurr. "Don't worry lad. It'll all be sorted soon," he said. "Until then, my missus is a great cook."

Someone brushed past me and I realised it was Mum. She looked at Gurr and then at Dad, who nodded. "No need for that, Inspector," she sighed. "No offence but I think Gurr would be happier among people who know him. So until his Mum and Dad come back... I suppose Gurr will just have to stay with us."

At that moment I was prouder of my parents than I'd ever been before.

Chapter 18

The next day I had to put worries about Buzby and Gurr out of my head. We were playing in the Schools Rugby Cup Final and, as captain, it was important I stayed focussed.

The game was at the local sports stadium with proper stands from which fans could show their support. There was a good-sized crowd with supporters from both schools, and I spotted a group of classmates who cheered and whooped when I led the team onto the pitch. Mum, Dad and Gurr were sitting further back, rows of empty seats all around them. With Gurr's suspension, lies in the newspaper and rumours about the Aggers' arrest, it was obvious that people were staying well clear. I waved to them and they waved back.

Dressed in our new kit and enjoying the cheers of our fans, we tossed balls to each other, practiced kicks and sprinted up and down the touchline. Despite getting to bed past midnight, I felt great. I knew we had an excellent team and had reached the final pretty easily. I stared proudly at the electronic scoreboard which displayed the day's fixture – Carson Street Juniors vs Mangate Juniors. This was the first time Carson Street had reached the final and I was confident we would win. At least I was confident until the Mangate team appeared.

They were huge. Every single one of them was taller, broader and heavier than us. They looked stronger and fitter. At least one of them had the beginnings of a wispy beard. Like a squad of well-drilled marines they marched forward and halted at the edge of the pitch. Their teacher walked down the line, nodding his approval. When he spoke, his voice echoed through the stadium.

"Who are we?"

The shouted reply was immediate and deafening. "We are Mangate."

"What are we?"

"We are the best."

"Why are we here?"

"To win."

"When will we win?"

"Noooowwww!"

Their response became a war cry, yelled at the tops of their voices as they stormed onto the pitch, bowling over any of our team who got in their way. I had a sudden urge to go to the toilet. Preferably one as far away from here as possible.

I turned from the army of giant trolls to my teammates. Shaun stood frozen, with his mouth open. Connor shuffled slowly backwards and moved behind Aiden as if for protection. Blake stared at the Mangate players and shook his head, softly repeating the word 'no' under his breath. Other team members stood in despair, hands on their heads. One by one they turned to face me.

As captain it was part of my job to boost my players' confidence, to encourage them, motivate them, inspire them. But right now I didn't feel particularly motivational or inspirational. The only advice I could think of while staring at our monstrous opposition was, 'Do your best, and try not to die'. At least I had the good sense not to say it out loud.

Mr Davies waved us over. He could see our worried faces and shrugged. "I've checked their ages and they're all eligible," he said. "But just because they're bigger than you, it doesn't mean they're better than you. The bigger they are, the harder they fall."

"If one falls on me I'll be crushed," Raphael said.

"Remember the story of David and Goliath?" Mr Davies said. "Goliath was huge and David was tiny, but David hit Goliath in the head with a rock and won the fight."

Blake brightened. "Does that mean we can throw rocks at them, sir?"

"No," I said. I had to raise their spirits. If we went onto the pitch feeling like this, we'd be beaten before the game even started. "The point is we can win this game if we believe we can and we all do our best. Look at them. If anything, they're too big. They'll be slow and clumsy. It'll be like a team of elephants against a team of cheetahs. We'll run rings around them."

They didn't look convinced. I tried again. "We're not scared of them! Who are we?"

The response was patchy and unenthusiastic. "Carson Street Juniors."

"What are we?"

There were blank looks and the odd, flat response, "We're the best."

"Why are we here?"

"To get our heads kicked in?" Blake ventured.

I raised my voice to a shout. I was the captain. I would be motivational. "When will we win?"

The team refused to be inspired. "Not today," Shaun said. The rest muttered their agreement.

I was saved from giving any more rousing speeches by the referee waving us onto the pitch. The teams took up their positions and I walked to the centre. Their captain eyed me hungrily, like a lion that hadn't had any dinner, and had just spotted a wounded zebra. I braced myself for the game ahead. It was going to be hard but I had to lead by example. If I showed I wasn't scared maybe the rest wouldn't be either.

The referee blew his whistle to start the game. Blake kicked off and I ran as fast as I could. The ball was caught by a Mangate forward and I was onto him before he had a chance to react. I tackled him hard, knocking him to the ground, but he managed to get the ball to a teammate and, as the game moved away, he punched me in the stomach.

I fell to my knees, retching, tears streaming down my cheeks. Cold air wheezed in and out of my lungs as I tried to control my breathing and dispel the sharp pain in my guts. I knelt there, panting, until the pain slowly subsided to a dull ache then managed to stand unsteadily. Through bleary eyes I looked down the pitch. The Mangate team still had the ball and were running for our line. Their captain took a pass, barged past our full-back, and scored a try.

I sighed. We were going to be massacred.

Chapter 19

Incredibly, I'd been right about elephants and cheetahs. The Mangate lads were bigger than us but they weren't faster and our speed kept us in the game. Once we'd gotten over the initial shock, we buckled down. I went over for a try, Blake scored with the goal kick, and we managed to keep their score down by determination and hard tackling.

Mangate were leading 11-7 with just minutes to go, but if we could score one try that would give us five points which would put us in the lead. It wouldn't be easy though. Mangate had played dirty since the kick off and had punched, kicked and stamped our players every time the referee's back was turned.

Harry was carried off after ten minutes and replaced by Aiden, who was also carried off five minutes later. We lost Charles with concussion just before half time, and Shaun with a split lip straight after. Wahab had just limped off with an ankle sprain, when their full-back stamped on my leg and a blinding pain hit me like an electric shock. Bright lights flashed before my eyes and the world spun, and suddenly Mr Davies was there examining my bleeding leg and applying a cold compress.

"It's not broken," he said. "But it'll hurt for a while. Come on."

He helped me hobble to the bench where I slumped in my seat with the rest of my shattered teammates. Gradually the pain subsided to a dull throb, the world stopped pretending I was on a fairground ride, and I was able to think again. I called to Mr Davies who was standing at the edge of the pitch, hands on his hips.

"Who's coming on?"

"No one," Mr Davies said, turning his head. "We've run out of substitutes. There's nobody left."

"But we must have somebody. We could still win."

Mr Davies shook his head. "I've asked the lads in the crowd. They're all eligible to play," he said. "But it seems a lot of old injuries have suddenly resurfaced... muscle problems, twisted ankles..."

"Then I'll go back on." I stood up and the pain, which had merely been in hiding, sent an agonising stab of warning to my brain. I sat down again and glanced up at our supporters, but not one of them would catch my eye. "Chickens!" I shouted.

A hand pulled at my sleeve and I turned to see Gurr standing behind me with Mum at his side.

"Play," he said.

Mr Davies frowned. "Play?"

"He insisted," Mum said.

"Oh, I'm not... that is, I don't think... if I... mmm!" Mr Davies stammered. The team definitely needed another player on the pitch, but Gurr?

"You can't play, Gurr," I said. "One strong tackle and your arms and legs will fall off. I mean, it's good that you offered but..."

"Play!" Gurr insisted.

Mr Davies spread his hands in an 'I don't know what to do' gesture. Gurr had a determined look in his red-rimmed eyes that I'd not seen before and I suddenly realised that, even as captain, I didn't have the right to stop him going on. He might be suspended, but he was a student at the school and he wanted to help. I called on Aiden to give Gurr his shirt. On Gurr's slight frame it looked like a baggy dress.

"Just be careful," I said.

Mr Davies indicated to the referee that he had a substitute.

The referee spotted Gurr. "Him?" he said.

Mr Davies shrugged, so the referee called Gurr onto the pitch.

A groan went up from our supporters as Gurr trotted to join the game, his awkward and distinctive running style bringing howls of laughter from the Mangate fans. But the Mangate captain wasn't amused. He waved to his teammates and shouted instructions, which consisted of three words.

"Get the freak!"

Chapter 20

There were only a couple of minutes to go, and so far the Mangate players had ignored their captain's instructions to 'get the freak'. If anything they had avoided Gurr, and his presence seemed to unnerve them. They obviously knew the rumours about Gurr and his family, and were not taking any chances of getting bitten. I was glad. We weren't going to win now and I just wanted Gurr to come off without injury.

Then the Mangate fly-half got the ball and kicked it across the field. It bounced once, straight into Gurr's arms. He stared at the ball as if he'd never seen one before. Most of the Mangate team didn't move and, for a moment, I wondered if they would allow Gurr to walk right past them. Then the Mangate captain and two of his braver forwards came running in to tackle.

"Gurr! Get rid of the ball!"

I shouted a warning but Gurr just stood there. A moment later he disappeared under the three players. When the mountain of bodies collapsed, the Mangate captain struggled out with the ball tucked securely under one arm and raced for our line. Everyone in the Carson Street team chased after him. Except Gurr.

Gurr got slowly to his feet. There were gasps from the crowd as he stood up. His head was gone. From the bulge at his chest it seemed it had somehow been pushed under his shirt, and now he walked, headless, in the opposite direction to everyone else. Some in the crowd groaned with horror, while others thought it was hilarious.

The Mangate full-back, his face drained of colour, edged away from Gurr, never taking his eyes from the terrible apparition. Walking backwards he stumbled over the uneven turf and fell onto his bottom. That broke the spell. With a yelp of terror he leapt back to his feet and ran.

At the other end of the pitch the Mangate captain dived for the line. He pulled the ball from under his arm to put it down for a try, and that was when he screamed. Because the rugby ball wasn't a rugby ball. It was Gurr's head.

"Uuuugh!" The Mangate captain's face crumpled with disgust as he tossed the head in the air and stood, his whole body shaking frantically, as if someone had poured a bucket of ants down his shirt.

Players from both sides stood around in shocked confusion. They might have heard of zombies' body parts coming off, but this was the first time most of them had witnessed it. A few of the more adventurous players slowly approached the discarded head, then shrieked as Gurr's eyes opened. There was a gurgle of zombie laughter and a voice, even croakier than usual, spoke.

"Got. Yu."

That was when realisation began to dawn. If the Mangate captain had Gurr's head then Gurr must have...

"Run!" I shouted. "Gurr! Run!"

Gurr pulled the rugby ball from under his shirt and began to run, his left leg windmilling while his right skipped and danced to keep pace.

The crowd picked up on what was happening before the players, and the Mangate fans were soon yelling at their team to chase Gurr. The brighter players quickly got the message and set off in pursuit.

Gurr was a good fifty metres in front of the chasing pack, but he was slow and awkward, and I knew if he tried to go faster a foot or even a leg could fly off at any time, and then it would be over.

"Run!" I screamed, hobbling down the touchline in excitement. "Run!"

Gurr was almost at the try line, the ball held precariously between his hands. The Mangate team were eating up the distance between them, but I could see they weren't going to catch him. I jumped up and down, the pain in my leg forgotten. Then Gurr stumbled, and fell.

The leading pursuers roared in triumph, as Gurr staggered to his feet. He was almost at the try line when the first Mangate player tackled him from behind and knocked him to the ground. I watched in despair as two others jumped on top. Gurr had been caught.

The hooter went for the end of the game.

I groaned with disappointment. Gurr had been so close. It would've been a brilliant try. It would've given us the five points we needed. We would've been champions. But Gurr had been caught and we'd lost. That was that. I was more concerned now to know Gurr was all right.

I limped across the pitch, where some of the Carson Street team had already started pulling the Mangate players off Gurr. As I approached, I could see the referee studying the ruck of bodies closely and, as more of Gurr was revealed, I understood why. The first tackle had carried Gurr forward and over the line. He was still holding the ball. The ball was on the ground.

The referee nodded, stood up straight, and blew his whistle. Gurr had scored the try.

We'd won.

Chapter 21

With screams of delight, me and my teammates leapt up and down, waved our arms and hugged anyone wearing the same colour shirt. My leg still hurt, but somehow it didn't matter. We were the champions!

Blake and Charles hoisted Gurr onto their shoulders, and carried our headless hero down the pitch. I hobbled behind, as best I could, laughing as Gurr waved to a crowd he could not see.

The Mangate team surrounded the referee, furiously complaining about the result. Their teacher held Gurr's head and shook it at the official.

"You can't have bits of players' bodies falling off and pretending to be rugby balls," he yelled. "It's not right. It's not hygienic."

"There's nothing against it in the rules," the referee said calmly.

"I'll have that." Mr Davies took hold of Gurr's head. The other teacher held on, glaring at Mr Davies, then seemed to think better of it and let go. Gurr winked and poked out his tongue.

"You little…" the teacher snorted and made a grab for Gurr's head. Luckily Mr Davies was too quick and whipped it out of reach before passing it to me.

Last time I'd held Gurr's head, it had felt weird and creepy. Now as I looked into his strange, smiling face it felt almost normal. He laughed and so did I.

Blake and Charles lowered Gurr, and I stuck his head onto his neck before they lifted him high again and carried on with their lap of honour. When we reached our supporters, the noise was deafening. Mum and Dad were cheering, and our schoolmates came running down from the stands to join the celebrations. They swarmed onto the pitch, laughing and shouting and crowding around Gurr to offer comment and congratulations.

"That was brilliant!"

"Amazing!"

"Did you see their faces?"

"Genius!"

A few of them pestered Gurr to take his head off again, which he did. Some of them squealed, but it was the kind of 'fun horror' squeal that people make in ghost houses or while watching scary movies. No one seemed afraid of Gurr, or horrified by him. It's amazing how a bit of success can change people's view of someone. Just a short while earlier Gurr had been a feared and unpopular outcast. Now, among his schoolmates at least, Gurr was a hero and he was happy to accept the adulation.

When things calmed down a little, we were presented with the cup and our medals, while the Mangate team looked on. Their captain was still shaking and a couple of them were in tears. The rest just scowled. They looked smaller and a lot more pathetic than the invincible team of ogres that had started the game. Despite myself, I felt a bit sorry for them. Then a sharp pain in my leg reminded me of how they had tried to punch and kick us out of the game. I turned to face the rest of my team.

"Who are we?" I asked loudly.

My teammates broke into huge grins and laughter. "We are Carson Street Juniors."

"What are we?"

They were loving this. "We are the best," they roared.

"Why are we here?"

Blake raised the cup high above his head. "To win."

"When did we win?

"Noooowwww!"

The team screamed in unison, jumping up and down and waving their medals in the air. Connor and Aidan each had an arm around Gurr's shoulders as they all bounced around, laughing and tunelessly singing victory songs.

It was great to see Gurr happy again and, as I watched the celebrations, I thought with a grin what a pity it was that Laura wasn't here to see it. She would have been furious.

What I didn't realise was that Laura had one more surprise in store for us.

Chapter 22

Me and Gurr wore our medals proudly, even after we'd changed and were leaving the ground. Mum and Dad met us by the car, gave me a hug and told me I'd played brilliantly. I hadn't, but it was still nice to hear. Then Dad turned to Gurr.

"That thing you did with your head," he said. "Good thinking, that."

"Thnk," Gurr said.

Mum twitched Gurr a weak smile and we stood awkwardly for a moment. Then she opened the car door. "Better drive you home," she said.

Me and Gurr climbed into the back and all the way home I talked through the game, describing every move, every tackle and score, ending with Gurr's incredible try. Gurr just listened and nodded occasionally. After a while I realised the excitement of the game had worn off for Gurr, and he was thinking about his parents.

"Wait until your Mum and Dad see your medal," I said. "I can't wait to tell them how amazing you were."

Gurr smiled that black-toothed smile of his, but I could see his heart wasn't in it.

As the car turned into our road, Gurr let out a cry. Outside his house stood a police car. Next to the police car stood Inspector McKeown. Next to the inspector stood Mr and Mrs Agger.

Mum applied the brakes and Gurr was out almost before we'd stopped. He ran to his parents who dropped to their knees to envelop him in a long, emotional hug. At last they moved apart and Mrs Agger stood up. She planted a kiss on top of Gurr's head, yipped a little bark then turned to us.

"Gurr. Stay. You," she said. "Thank."

Mum coughed to clear her throat. The affectionate reunion had obviously touched her, even though she didn't want to admit it. "That's all right," she said, brushing a tear from her cheek. "He's a... lovely boy."

Mr Aggers' lip curled like a hyena about to take a lump out of a buffalo carcass and he advanced on Dad, who took a step back.

"It's OK, Dad," I said. "He's smiling."

Mr Agger nodded and a low growl rumbled in his chest as he put out his hand.

"Thnk," he said.

"Right. Yes," Dad shook the hand quickly and let go.

Mr Agger took a step back and straightened his wig which had slipped over one ear. Everyone nodded and smiled, and we might have stood there for some time not knowing what else to do if the inspector hadn't eventually spoken. He addressed Mum and Dad.

"No charges were brought," he said. "Your son's statement and other witnesses cleared the Aggers of assault in town. A search of the house has shown no evidence of animals ever being in there, and there's no evidence the Aggers ever touched the bin bag or any of the collars in it." He turned to Gurr, suddenly serious. "But I have bad news for you, lad."

Gurr looked suddenly worried.

"Your head teacher's an old friend of mine. We've talked and, in light of my investigation, he agrees that the whole rabbit thing was probably just a misunderstanding. He wants you back in school tomorrow."

Now that might have been bad news for some kids, but not for Gurr. He gave a gurgled cheer and punched the air so hard his hand shot off, showering him with a faint spray of brown goo. Inspector McKeown, with surprising skill, caught the hand on its downward arc and passed it back to Gurr who nodded his thanks.

Mum's face crinkled in revulsion as Gurr snapped the hand back onto his wrist. "So, they really are safe then?" she asked.

"Yes," the inspector said. "The virus took away some of their intellect and language skills, and there were some obvious physical changes, but yes, they really are safe."

Mr and Mrs Agger shook the inspector's hand again, nodded in our direction and walked back to the house with Gurr. At the gate Gurr stopped, held up his medal and waved for me to join them. I glanced at Mum.

She stood in silence for a moment, staring at the Aggers. Then she sighed. "Just don't stay there all day," she said at last. "Your tea'll be ready at five."

Grinning, I gave Mum a peck on the cheek and limped off to catch up with Gurr. He draped a bony arm around my shoulder and we walked up to the house. Gurr had his parents back, all charges against them were dropped, his suspension was lifted, he was popular at school again and he had a friend who could visit his house. This was turning out to be Gurr's best day ever.

Then the howling mob arrived.

Chapter 23

"Zombies out! Zombies out! Zombies out!"

A group of men and women came marching down the street, shaking their fists and shouting. Some were waving League Against Zombie banners. As they drew closer I recognised the short, fat man in the red bow tie at the front of the crowd. It was Laura's dad. His face was flushed and his eyes were puffy, as if he'd been crying.

The inspector, talking urgently into his radio, strode to meet the crowd.

"They've got my Laura," Mr Mosley yelled, as the inspector drew near. "They've got my beautiful little girl!"

I shook my head in disbelief. This was obviously another one of Laura's tricks to make Gurr look bad and now she had half the estate on her side. I was about to tell them not to believe anything Mr Mosley said, when he spotted the Aggers.

"Get 'em!" he roared.

The crowd surged in our direction, some jumping over the fence, others shoving through the gate. I saw the inspector and Mum and Dad try to get between us and the mob, but there were too many of them. I pushed Gurr and his parents into the house, and slammed and locked the door.

"Come on!" I shouted, grabbing Gurr by the arm.

Fortunately, the design of the house was exactly the same as my own. I pulled Gurr through the kitchen and out through the back door, his parents following. We'd just reached the cover of bushes to the rear of the garden when some of the protestors came around the corner and started banging on the back door. There was a crash of breaking glass as someone hurled a rock through a window. I signalled for the Aggers to stay quiet and we crept away. A moment later we were in the Jungle.

"It won't take them long to realise you're not in there," I whispered. "We have to go."

"Not. Do. Any. Thing," Gurr's Mum said, her voice shaking.

"I know you haven't done anything. But they'll come after you." I took her hand. It felt cold and brittle. "Please. I know where we can hide."

Mrs Aggers' eyes flashed angrily. She gave a sharp yip and turned to face the way we'd come. It was clear Mrs Agger wasn't one to be pushed around. She intended to stand and fight.

Mr Agger moved in front of her. "Prtct Grr," he said. "Bst way. Hide."

Mrs Agger growled and stood rocking on her feet like a boxer ready for the bell. Then, slowly, the tension seemed to seep from her body. She turned and looked at me. "Hide?"

I nodded. "Hide."

Mrs Agger barked, as if in protest, but followed when I started to run down the narrow dirt track. I led them along paths and unmarked trails, but even with my bad leg I still had to stop to let them catch up. Mr and Mrs Aggers' running style was no better than Gurr's. They wobbled and stumbled in a way that would have been funny if the situation wasn't so serious.

We were moving too slowly. I could hear the sound of the mob behind us. They'd found the house empty and were now crashing through the woods. From the closeness of their shouts, they would be on us in seconds.

Chapter 24

"In here!"

I pulled back a drooping branch covered in thick foliage to reveal a small gap in the undergrowth. Gurr recognised it at once, dropped to his knees and crawled inside. His Mum and Dad followed without hesitation, and I went last. We crept through the small tunnel of twisted shrubbery until we emerged into the den. It was a tight fit with all of us there, but it was warm and surprisingly comfortable.

We sat in silence, listening as the noise of the mob grew nearer. I felt a vibration on my arm and realised it was Mr Agger, pressed against me and growling softly. I nudged him and shook my head. He grunted, but the growling stopped.

Through gaps in the leaves I saw shadows move and figures emerge from the woods. They were so close I could have pushed my hand through the branches and touched them. I watched Mr Mosley stab a finger at Dad.

"She was coming to… see a friend. But she never turned up," he shouted. "Since then she hasn't answered her phone. Those monsters have eaten her! I know they have!"

I knew that wasn't true as Laura didn't have any friends nearby. If she had come to this part of the estate it would have been to cause trouble for the Aggers. Mr Mosley must have known that, or he wouldn't be accusing them.

"Don't be daft," I heard Mum say. "Gurr's been with us at the rugby and his mum and dad were with the police. She's probably gone to the shops with her mates."

"No! She always answers her phone. Something's happened to her." Tears ran freely down Mr Mosley's face and at that moment I felt sorry for him. If this was a trick of Laura's, it was an especially cruel one to make her own dad suffer like that.

"Right, you lot, listen to me!" came a voice that was deep and commanding. "I want everybody here, now!"

Inspector McKeown emerged from the trees and stood waiting for the rest of the mob to appear, which they did in ones and twos. "Some of you," he said loudly, his words carrying through the woods, "are guilty of threatening behaviour and criminal damage and I will deal with you later. But right now we have a missing child. We know that Laura left home at about three o'clock. If she was coming here it's likely she would have caught the thirty-three bus, which meant she could have cut through the Jungle."

Mr Mosley seemed to shrink in on himself. "I told her not to go into the woods," he said softly.

The inspector put a comforting hand on his shoulder. "We've got a lot of people here," he said. "So, instead of harassing innocent citizens, why don't we find your daughter? Right! You lot," he pointed to a group of men, who were hanging back amongst the trees. "Come with me. The rest of you, with the sergeant."

The crowd moved away, the inspector giving orders until his voice faded and it was silent apart from the occasional tweet of a bird and the rustle of leaves in the light wind.

Sitting in the den, I was reminded of when Gurr and I had hidden there before. I thought about the conversation we'd overheard. We'd known then that one of the men was Mr Mosley, but I hadn't given much thought to his companion. Now, as I replayed the conversation in my mind, I realised with a sudden shock that I recognised the other man's voice. I knew who he was, and I knew exactly what he'd been talking about.

"Lstn!" Gurr's whisper interrupted my thoughts. I listened. At first there was nothing, then I heard what could have been a faint cry. We waited, then it came again.

"It could be a trick," I said.

"Need. Hlp," Gurr said simply and crawled out of the den.

Chapter 25

We all followed Gurr out of our hiding place and, once in the open, I looked around nervously. The inspector had cleared the mob but I still expected them to appear at any moment. Gurr set off walking with the rest of us close behind. The cry was clearer now. It was someone shouting for help and it was directly ahead.

"Stop!" I whispered, grabbing Gurr's arm. He stopped. "Listen."

The cries were now mingled with other sounds, people talking and shouting. I moved in front of the others and, as quietly as I could, pushed through the undergrowth. After a few steps I held up one hand to signal for silence, then gently pulled the overgrown branches aside. I peered through at a clearing. Milling around were some of the people that had attacked the Aggers' house. Mr Mosley was there and so were Mum and Dad, but what caught my attention was Laura. She was crying, shouting for help and stuck up to her shoulders in a thick bog.

"Help! Get me out!" she sobbed. "I'm sinking!"

"I'm coming!" A frantic Mr Mosley ran straight into the mire, but only managed a few steps before he was stuck up to his knees and couldn't move any further. Friends grabbed him and, with some difficulty, pulled him free. Around Laura, bubbles burbled as she sank a little further, releasing a rank smell of rotting vegetation.

The inspector appeared, listening to his radio. "The fire service is on its way," he said to Mr Mosley. "We'll soon have her out. You'll see." But his voice wasn't as confident as usual. I could see he was worried. "Pull that branch down!"

A couple of men tugged and swung on a long branch until it snapped under their weight and they fell to the ground in a shower of twigs and leaves. The inspector lifted the branch and laid it out over the bog. "Hold on and I'll pull you out," he called to Laura.

"I can't," she wept. "My arms are stuck." She struggled and the quagmire squelched as she sank to her neck.

The inspector knelt to examine the branch. It was long enough to reach Laura but, if she couldn't grab it, it was useless. "Hold my legs," he said and eased himself onto the surface of the bog. With people holding on, the inspector half-swam and half-crawled. He stretched out one arm, straining to reach Laura, but with every movement sank a little further until it became clear he was never going to make it without drowning himself. Without waiting to be told, those helping dragged the inspector back to the safety of firm ground where he sat, panting, his head bowed.

The bog belched a large bubble and Laura sank further. The rancid swamp now covered her chin. Her eyes widened in terror. Mr Mosley sank to his knees. "Please! Somebody do something!" he pleaded.

Gurr whispered to his parents and they nodded. Together they pushed past me and stepped into the clearing. I expected immediate uproar, with the mob attacking the Aggers as soon as they saw them, but they didn't. Maybe it was because of Laura, stuck in the mire. Maybe it was because they realised that the Aggers weren't responsible for her disappearance after all.

"We. Hlp," Gurr's dad said, and pulled off both of Gurr's mum's arms.

There were screams and some of the mob turned and ran. Others stood rooted to the spot in shock. Appalled at the unprovoked attack by Mr Agger on his own wife, Inspector McKeown jumped to his feet.

"What the…?"

"S'OK," Gurr's mum said. "Watch."

The inspector hesitated as Mr Agger positioned his wife's long, stringy arms, so that one hand was holding the other's bicep. Gurr rolled up his sleeves and pulled off one of his arms. His mum's hand grabbed it. Mr Agger held out the chain of arms like a bizarre fishing rod across the bog, towards Laura. It was just short.

"One. Mre," Gurr said, turning to me. For a moment I didn't know what he meant then he lifted his remaining arm.

"You want me to… pull it off?"

Gurr nodded. "Pll."

My stomach churned. I didn't want to pull Gurr's arm off. I'd barely got used to him doing it, but me? I couldn't. I wouldn't. I was suddenly aware of someone standing next to me. It was my dad.

"Do you want me to do it?"

I shook my head. Gurr was my friend. He'd asked me. But…

"Please," Mr Mosley cried. "Please. She's sinking."

That did it. I took a deep breath, and a firm hold around Gurr's upper arm, and pulled. There was a horrible, squelching sound as the joint separated, and a jolt, and I was left holding a dismembered arm. Gurr's other arm swung my way and the hand tugged the limb out of my grasp.

Mr Agger walked to the edge of the mire, dangling the linked arms ahead of him. It was more than enough to reach Laura. At the end of the chain, Gurr's hand dropped close to Laura's face. It dripped a blob of brown gloop onto her nose. She screamed.

"Get it away! Get it away!"

Gurr's hand moved around the back of Laura's head and grabbed her collar. Gurr's dad pulled his wife's left arm, which pulled on her right arm, which pulled on Gurr's left arm, which pulled on his right arm, which pulled on Laura. For a moment it seemed as if nothing would happen. Then there was a squirt and a squelch and a bubble and a burp as the bog released its hold. Slowly, very slowly, Laura was dragged across the swamp and onto land.

Covered in an oozing layer of black slime from her neck down, Laura lay panting for breath. Mr Mosley ran to embrace her, then stopped dead. A terrible pong was rising off his daughter like a thick fog. He retched and took a step backwards, as did everyone else.

Gurr wrinkled his nose and pulled a face at Laura. "Yu stnk," he said.

The mob, which only minutes earlier had been ready to attack the Aggers, now looked confused. Despite what the inspector had said, they believed the Aggers to be dangerous, but now they'd seen them rescue a child from the bog. And what's more, a child who hated them. They didn't know what to think, so the inspector helped to make up their minds.

"The Agger family are not dangerous," he said, scooping thick handfuls of sludge from his uniform. "You've seen that for yourselves. So now, I think you should all go home."

"Not yet," I shouted. "Before you go, you need to see something else. Everybody, follow me."

Chapter 26

Despite the ache in my leg, I ran down the dirt track and out of the Jungle. A quick glance back assured me that the others were following. I ran down the street and around a corner to a house just a few minutes from my own. I marched up the path and thumped on the door. After a moment it opened and Mr Webster appeared. In jeans and an old t-shirt he looked very different from the smart teacher I normally saw at school.

"Laura? About time. I…"

"You said your house was starting to stink," I said. "I didn't realise who it was then or what it meant, but I do now."

At first Mr Webster looked puzzled, then angry. "How dare you?" he said then froze as he noticed the inspector and a flurry of police cars arrive. His face went pale and his legs seemed to collapse. He grabbed onto the door for support, and by the time the inspector joined me Mr Webster was babbling.

"I didn't hurt them," he said. He pointed at Laura, whom someone had thoughtfully wrapped in a blanket. As she walked she dripped a trail of slime like a giant, bog-covered slug. "She helped me to look after them. She'll tell you." Then he spotted Mr Mosley. "It was his fault! He made me do it! He said it would get rid of the freaks! He's to blame!"

Caught between looking after his daughter and escaping, Mr Mosley hesitated then ran. He barged through the crowd of people like a Mangate forward, knocking his recent supporters aside. Mum took a step back to get out of his way, but as he passed she stuck out a foot. Mr Mosley tripped, flew into the air and crashed to the ground. Within seconds, two burly police officers jumped on him and had his arms handcuffed behind his back.

Two more officers gripped the protesting Mr Webster by each arm, and marched him to a police car. I moved to let them pass then pushed open the door. The inspector followed me into the teacher's living room, where we were hit with a sharp smell of wee, fur and damp sawdust. All the usual furniture had been removed and, along each wall, stacks of cages were piled high. In each cage was an animal. There were cats, dogs, rabbits, guinea pigs – all of the pets that were missing from the estate. And in one cage a Yorkshire Terrier began barking and leaping madly around his confined space. It was Buzby. I opened the cage and he jumped into my arms, licking my face with sloppy dog kisses.

So that was it. Mr Webster was arrested and charged with theft and criminal damage. Mr Mosley faced the same charges, plus a couple of extra ones of threatening behaviour and actual bodily harm for pulling off Gurr's ear. Mr Webster lost his job and, after the trial, Mr Mosley and his family moved far away. Best of all, everyone knew that the Aggers hadn't harmed Laura or eaten people's pets.

The local newspaper loved the story, of course, despite what they'd printed the week before. Gurr framed the front page of the Chronicle and it hangs on his bedroom wall. The headline reads, 'Everyone agrees, local zombies are 'armless.' Beneath the story is a photograph of the Aggers and I'm in the picture too, holding Buzby and standing next to Gurr, my zombie best friend.

THE END